AMUSEMENT PARK

CHUONG VAN NGUYEN

SWEETSPIRE LITERATURE
MANAGEMENT

nce upon a time, there were students from High school that were invited to go on a trip to the amusement park in an unknown location, they were selected and chosen by this strange looking mystery girl new to the school which everybody thought that she was. On the day she was going around handing out free invitation tickets to students without saying a single word to them. Nearly everybody was wondering who she was and where she came from. Some of the students think she resembles a horror movie based on her appearance. The ones that had gotten the invitation from her find her quite to be disturbing due to her looks and some of the others find her to look quite cool.

The mystery girl went around handing out to most of the students until lucky last one that she gave and chose, his name was "Danny!"

He didn't know what to say at first, but he too was the only one to ask of her what her name is, and she told him that her name is "Matilda!" and walks away at a fast pace.

The rest of the others didn't really care much about who she was or where she'd come from.

When she gave the last invitation to him, she was no longer to be seen at the school again that day.

Danny's close friend named Michael also received the invitation as well.

They both opened together the enveloped and saw what the invitation was about, and it explained to them the meet-up location of the "amusement park" specially chosen for them. It further explains, that everybody will get a bonus at the end of the game.

"Doesn't sound like an ordinary theme park to me, Michael said!" in a fascinating way.

Therefore, it shows the time and date for them to arrive there. Which is the next morning sharp on a Saturday!

Michael just couldn't stop thinking as to why this all sounds weird to him, such as himself and the others are getting free tickets and such on.

Danny thinks this is probably like all the other amusement parks that he has been to. "Nothing usual, he says!"

That afternoon, while everybody is going home from school, Michael and Danny are walking together and talking until suddenly Danny sees a weird clown holding a balloon standing from a distance to them at a nearby tree waving.

He asks his friend Michael does he sees that clown from a distance. He told him no; he didn't see it. He doesn't see any clown anywhere.

Danny then turned his head back and looked but see no clown anywhere?

"You must be delusional to be seeing things, Michael said!" in a joking way. A CLOWN!

"Nah, your probably right, Danny replies!" I am probably seeing things. I thought I saw a clown that resembles a horror movie "The it" if you have watched that.

"It was one of my scary horror icons since I was a child, and it gave me chills. I had the fear of him ever since I could remember my childhood and couldn't sleep properly."

"It's alright, you'll get over it, said Michael!"

Michael's wonders if Danny's school crush would also be going as well to the theme park.

When he asked that question to him, out of nowhere Danny's crush appeared. Her name was Jessica. She too is also with her close friend named Jane.

The two Jessica and Jane both walked together across passed Danny and Michael.

"There goes your girl, Michael said!"

Jessica walks by smiling at Danny, and he too smiles back and waves at her. She notices it and continues walking off.

Danny asks her in a loud tone voice from the distance to them if she had received the invitation and is going to the amusement park on a Saturday.

She replied, yes!

Her friend said yes also that she's coming too if anybody is interested, like that if anybody cares.

"That's great," Danny continues to speak out loud to them! while they're walking away.

After that, Michael asks Danny if he would like to go to his party later this evening due to the end of the weekdays.

"Sure, why not, said he!"

They suddenly went both their separate ways and headed back home preparing for the after party.

During that time of the evening, the party had already commenced at Michael's house, while Danny is still at his house getting dressed and ready to go.

About an hour later, Danny had finally arrived at the party. He was a little bit upset to see that the party had already started without him.

There was packed with people from his school that had already started the fun.

Michael just stood there and looked at him telling him to relax by cheering him up knowing that the party had already started early without him.

He was all cheered up, and ready to have some fun. He asks Michael a question about his mom and dad, "where are they?"

Michael explains to him that his family is having a sleepover at their relatives for the night, which there is no need to worry about.

"You did the party without even your parents knowing about it, said him?"

He didn't care less about it and neither did he. They both just went ahead and enjoyed the party.

While Danny and Michael were partying with the others, more people came along knocking on his door. They let them in.

After having fun drinking and getting tipsy, Danny notices and sees Matilda and a clown that he saw earlier standing in the crowd, distance from him. He ask Michael to look and see if he saw it too, but he didn't see.

Danny looks again at the same position where they were standing and sees none of them there.

"I must be tripping, he said!" from all that drinking.

His friend tells him to forget about it, then they both continue partying with the rest of the others. They were having so much fun that the time passed by eventually until it was almost morning when sunlight could be seen rising from the sky.

Michael notices it and so as Danny. He quickly tells the rest of the others to all leave his house so they can unpack the garbage bags and clean everything before his parents arrived back home.

When they all had left besides the two, they both were so hung over and exhausted from the partying, they had no choice but to clean up the entire house as soon as possible. Danny quickly told him to do it fast before his parents comes home and lecture him.

Moments later once that was done, they both cheered in victory for finishing off all the mess that they made. And out of nowhere they suddenly both started to vomit. They made a bit of a mess on the floor.

They both quickly moped it up clean. Michaels parents has arrived back home. Mom and Dad, both ask him how his night with his mate was. Everything is good, they replied.

Danny just remembered about the amusement park that they must go today and they're almost about to be late.

He quickly rushes him to finish talking to his parents, but he is also making second thoughts about it due to the tiredness of the party.

"My future wife is going to be there, said Danny!" Please come, as a friend. "Danny begs!"

He gave a thought about it for a moment and agreed to go and quickly rushed his mom and dad. The two went on their bikes and hurried as fast as they could.

When they were riding, they both got exhausted and were afraid they might be late to arrive there to the specific location to meet up where it was shown on the invitation.

When they have almost arrived at that spot, Danny told Michael from behind him that the waiting point is not that far from their school.

"It is just around the corner, he said!" which they didn't take notice of it when they were looking at it the on invitation card.

They could see the other students from a distance standing and waiting for the driver to come pick them up. They could also see Jessica and Jane as well.

Once they both arrived, they locked their bicycle chains to the pole nearby. They jogged up to where Jessica and Jane were standing.

Jessica waved a Hi at them two.

"Luckily the bus didn't come just yet, otherwise the both of you would have been late, said she!"

When Danny was about to speak to her back, the weird-looking carnival bus suddenly arrived to pick them up.

The students can be heard talking to each other that this is no ordinary bus and that they have never ever seen it before.

The door opens, and the students can see a driver to be a creepy looking unusual clown.

The clown bus driver's hand signals the students to all hop in the bus as he does not speak.

Everyone then went on.

While sitting peacefully, one of the students asks the bus driver how long the drive is going to be. But he did not respond and continued with his driving.

The student then felt awkward because of his ignorance and neglect, so he went back to sit on his seat.

While on the trip to the carnival, Danny is sleeping with his head rest backwards and Michael is sleeping leaning against Danny's shoulder. They both were so tired from last night partying.

Moments later, Danny suddenly wakes up in a panic mode which made Michael wake up as well.

"What happen, Michael asks!"

"I just had a nightmare, said Danny!" in a panic way.

"It is nothing, said Michael!" and it was only just a horrible dream.

But Danny told him something doesn't feel right about all this, especially going to this amusement park.

One of the students could overheard what he said and yelled out to everybody that Danny just had a wet dream. Suddenly all the students started to laugh.

Then everybody stops laughing for a second and can hear the bus driver laughing with a very unusual creepy voice. They stopped laughing because they had never heard his voice before up until now.

Everybody just looked next to each other thinking just how creepy and horrible his laugh sounds.

Michael asks Danny does the bus driver reminds him of the clown character from the movie "killer clowns from outer space."

"Yeah, he does kind of resembles one of them from that movie, Danny said!"

They both wonder why they see horror look alike from movies since yesterday and till now.

They're wondering why it's odd to be seeing something strange like this occur since Matilda showed up new to the school on the day.

Anyhow the other students complain about why the trip is taking so long. But there's nothing that can be done about it.

About moments later, all the students fell asleep including Danny and Michael again. The driver then beeps his horn for the students to wake up. They had finally arrived at the destination to the amusement park. Everybody got a jump scared of the sound of the horn.

The driver opened the door of the bus for the students to hop off. They all went out. The bus then drives away without saying anything.

Not that it matters the students didn't care less about him. Everybody was just happy that they had finally made it here.

They were all walking to the front entrance and into the amusement park.

The looks on the students' faces were filled with excitement. They had never seen any amusement park like this one before.

"This is not like any other ordinary theme parks that I have been too, said one of the students!" It feels and looks like we're in a nineteen fifty or sixties vibe.

When they were talking, the front entrance automatically closes. Nobody cared much about it, but Danny was the only one that was concerned about the place. something doesn't feel right about it that he kept on saying to Michael. But he told him to relax and have fun, it's Saturday and he is just spooked out because of his nightmare on the bus earlier.

One of the theme park attendances is announcing to the students to begin and have a "Hell of A Fun".

"Now this is going to be super fun, said Michael!" This is no ordinary theme park; everything is enormous and there are so many fun games to play and choose. It is going to take forever to finish.

Danny wonders why there are no other people around but just the people from his school are here.

While he is thinking about that, all the students are already heading off to the games that they see and are interested in.

The three, Michael, Jessica and Jane call out to him for being distracted by something, asking him to come with them to one of the games.

So, he came along with them. And while playing the games, so far, they're wondering why and how come the games are very super cheap to play, compared to all the other amusement parks that they had been to which are expensive.

But not that it really matters to them, they were just happy that everything was cheap. "A pop of soda is only ten cents, one of the four said!" which is amusingly cheap for now a day. The rides and games are amazingly only fifty cents a play, which is unbelievable.

"We could be playing and hanging around in here all night until morning with our money spent, said Jessica!"

"This isn't no regular theme park, said she!" in a very thrilled and fascinating way.

The four then just continuously went ahead and played all the games that they could see at their sights. They were very much enjoying themselves.

While playing most of the games, they head off and go onto the rollercoaster ride, but Danny isn't up for it. He is afraid of the ride because it is too fast and scary.

So, they all went to a different section instead. While walking to see where they should head next, they all see this place called the fun house. They decided to go in. They were having fun getting spooked out in the house encountering wild scary things.

They were having fun in there for a while, and when they had finished and went out of the house, they started to feel kind of hungry. They told each other that was one scary place that they had so far been to.

So, they head to the takeaway cart to buy something to eat. While the four were eating, Danny turns around and sees a midget clown behind him.

The little one speaks to him by asking him to come closer to him so he can whisper into his ears.

And as he did, the midget clown told him the real fun begins soon.

He magically throws a smoke ball and disappears without a trace.

Jane asks Danny who he was! and what did the midget clown want?

"He didn't say nothing much, said he!" all he said was "the real fun begins soon!"

And just when they were about to move on to the next game after finishing eating their food. A scary siren sound suddenly appears out of nowhere from the top tower.

Everybody just stood there quietly feeling confused and nervous as to why that siren is on for what reason.

About seconds later the siren stops, everybody was wondering what in the hell was that all about. They were frightened.

Then the others were looking around the area and saw nothing from the park was moving. Everything is all paused. Even the games and the attendance are paused. All the lights from the theme park suddenly went out and it got dark.

Everybody is freaking out not knowing what to do due to the darkness of the area. Until one of the students took out a cigarette lighter and lit it up. He had no choice but to burn his winning from earlier which was a rag doll to give out more light. Everybody can see much more clearly now.

They all went and gathered in a group. They were talking to one another, feeling scared.

The doll that was burnt by the student was then out of fire and it went back dark again, suddenly the lights of the amusement park went back on again.

Everything went back to normal, but the students noticed the attendance of the game sections have all disappeared.

"Something doesn't feel right about this, said Jessica!"

"This is what I've been trying to tell you guys about when I got here, said Danny!" in a scary panicking way.

This whole thing doesn't feel right but none of you guys cared what I say but cared more about having fun at the time when I explained earlier.

He tried to calm them down. He told everybody to head to the front entrance to exit the theme park knowing that something doesn't feel right.

When they all had almost gotten there to the front gate, they suddenly slowed down and stopped. They could see someone or something blocking and standing in their path at the near entrance. They got a closer look and saw a fancy clown standing there holding up a cardboard sign.

Jessica was the first to respond to it asking him for help and he did not respond back. So, she came up closer and looked and what she discovered to be nothing but a human size clown doll.

She takes extra steps towards it to check it out and so as the rest of the other students.

She grabs the cardboard out of the doll's hands to see what it has written on it.

"What does it say, Danny asks?"

"It says, what is each one of your scariest horror movie icons are since childhood."

Out of nowhere, all the students are saying out all their scary icons to each other until Jessica flips over the cardboard and sees there's more to it!

Congratulations! You will now meet your horror icons starting from now commencing in ten seconds.

She drops the cardboard from her hand with scared in vain. She and the others don't know what to do next.

Jessica and Jane were starting to cry, feeling scared and so thinking that this might be real after all.

"It doesn't matter, Danny says!" if this is real or not.

He further told everybody to go and find a place to hide and see what happens from there.

Running and escaping from the entrance is no good due to all the chains that had been locked up from the gate.

Danny quickly grabs Jessica's hand and makes a run for it to find a hiding spot for them. Everybody finds a spot. The countdown is over. The ten seconds are over, and nobody sees anything happening. Everybody is complaining about it.

but for a sudden out of nowhere, there were some strange sounds coming from around the gaming sections in the distance.

They can hear a much louder screeching sound from a closer range. They can also hear a familiar laugh as well.

"Don't tell me what I think it is, said Michael!" in a recognizing way.

Everybody can see someone lurking from the shadows popping out which looks like to be a human figure with razer claws on his right hand.

Michael looks extra closer to see who he thinks it is and is freaked out. He quietly whispers to the others telling them it's him, "Freddy Krueger!" "He is my main horror icon since my childhood!"

Then everybody can suddenly hear Freddy laughing. And another sound also can be heard from a different spot, a gurgling sound from a distance, and it sounds very familiar to Jessica, and she knows who that is. She said it belongs to Kayako Saeki from the grudge movie! Which was her scary icon since childhood.

Then Chucky from the child's play movie appeared out of nowhere and same goes to pennywise the dancing clown from "it" movie. Both horror icons belong to Danny and Jane.

And the rest of the other horror icons came out belonging to the other students.

Everybody suddenly started to scream in fear. All the students have made a run for it. They try to run away from their living nightmares.

While they were all running away, Michael's icon Freddy Krueger can be heard saying, "I can sense and smell your fear." "You can run but you can't hide!"

Michael stopped and couldn't barely move his body due to the fear of Freddy. So, Jane grabbed his arm, forcing him to run away with her. And when they ran, they went and found another quiet spot to hide. They were hiding there until Chucky came and appeared out of nowhere to them "Peek a boo!"

They both got a jump scare and ran off out of their hiding spot.

All the students were running around in fear don't know where to go or hide from their horror icons.

When everybody was running, the four bumped into each other again Danny, Jessica, Michael and Jane.

They didn't know what else to do and Danny tells the three to follow him as he tries to lead the way to somewhere where he can find safety.

While they were running away, they saw these mini fun houses and went to one of them to hide. When they all went in, they locked and blocked the door with a sledgehammer that was on the side so that no one could come in.

While they're busy doing that, they didn't take notice who was behind them when they first got into the mini fun house.

There is a chubby clown man sitting there tied up to a chair with socks in his mouth where he could not speak.

They didn't know what to expect and do next. They don't know whether they should untie or just leave him there.

Jessica came up to him and took out the socks from his mouth.

He thanked her for that as he could now properly breathe.

She asks him who is he and can he help them and why it is that he was tied up to a chair.

He didn't tell them his name or why he was tied up to a chair at first, but he further told them that he was willing to help them if they would untie him.

The four must assume he is a good person and is being tortured by the evil ones from this place due to all the bruises and blood which can be seen on him. So, they untie him with trust.

He thanked them again for that. He told the four to come with him and follow his league wherever he goes, starting from the backyard of this house where there is a toilet out back.

When they have gotten there, the chubby clown man lifts the carpet from the toilet room and there sees a tunnel that could lead them somewhere.

The chubby clown man obviously leads the way first telling them to follow him with trust because the others wasn't so sure what the tunnel would lead them to.

The tunnel looks dark and scary but with extra light bulbs hanging from the top.

They all entered. It took a while for them to get to the exit of the tunnel. Long moments of crawling, they have finally made it out. The chubby clown man told them to be quiet and walk in a very slow pace as it looks like they didn't make it that far out of this amusement park but still here, which looks to be a place where like to be in another game section of the park.

"We didn't go anywhere, said Jane!" that long travelling through the tunnels thought it would lead us outside, but we are still here. What's going on?

Jane feels something fishy about the chubby clown man where he led them to, but he looks innocent to them somehow.

"Where are you taking us, said she?"

"Don't worry just trust me and follow, said the chubby clown man!"

They were all tippy toeing to another game section where it is quiet in that location. They were hiding there for a moment. The chubby clown man told them to look at all the other students of theirs seeing what is happening to them.

They all witness something in their very own eyes, they witness something which is out of this world.

They see the rest of the other students being tortured at first and being dragged down by their horror icons into the ground hells portal.

They can hear the students scream in fear. They were screaming for help but nobody can help them.

While they were watching, the clown man explains to the four that once the horror icons of the students have taken them to hell, they are too the horror icons are also gone as well. They will no longer serve a purpose in this game and will no longer hurt or harm any other students.

When nearly all the students are been dragged down to hell, there are still only some students left remaining still on the run.

Danny asks the chubby clown man why or how he knows so much about this and wanted to also know how their horror icons can be killed and what did they do to deserve this, but the clown man didn't quite tell them exactly why they deserve this but told them that yes, their horror icons could be killed, and they could avoid going to hell. He further explains to the kids that he doesn't know why they have been dragged to hell when Danny continued asking him, because he did not answer his question properly. He noticed something very odd about him and was very precautious.

The chubby clown man explains if their horror icons are killed then they are set free which if they're brave enough to fight them!

Danny thought about it and came up with a strategy. He asks his group to all work together like in the movies to survive and beat this game in order to survive and win.

As so, everyone listens to him and follows his plan.

"A trap also must be made to succeed, said he!"

There is lots of electricity and cables in this theme park that could be used as weapons.

To eradicate the nightmare icons once and for all, Danny was the main lead guy and is further commanding the others how to kill them. he first explains to Jane that she can kill Chucky like nothing because its just a small size doll which can be killed easily just like in his child play movies.

"Go find a sledgehammer and beat the living crap out of him!" "Splatter him into pieces, said he!" in a confident way.

And as for Jessica, Danny told her to be brave and use a decoy on Kayako Saeki by telling her to keep on running around anywhere to buy themselves some time to create their trap with the chubby clown man.

And as for him and Michael's horror icons "Pennywise and Freddy". Danny makes Michael think of a trick for them into fighting each other by confusion.

So, each one of them listened and went ahead and did what he asked for them to survive.

In the time being, when all that had happened as they planned, Jane was the first to be successful at eliminating Chucky when she had already found the sledgehammer. She found him and killed him with it on an instant. His head was splattered into pieces.

While in the other hand, Jessica is still on the run from Kayako Saeki and as for Michael, he is caught up with the two Freddy Krueger and Pennywise the dancing clown. He is stalling the two around by tricking them, making fun of and telling lies about each other to make them hate and fight. And for the time being they could not take it anymore and fought each other.

"The plan worked said Michael!" in a very proud successful way!

He then quickly tells Danny and the chubby clown man to hurry up with his trap that he is setting up.

They're now complete. The trap is now done. Pennywise has also killed off Freddy at the time.

Michael went up to Danny and asks him who's this trap is set for? And he told him it's for only Jessica's horror icon. But since there are only two remaining left Pennywise and Kayako Saeki down for the count. We can lure both together and eliminate them.

Suddenly Jessica and Jane ran back and met up with the other two, Danny and Michael. They all stood together near the trap that Danny created and clown man.

Pennywise and Kayako Saeki are walking slowly towards them to capture Jessica and Danny to drag them down to hell.

The five were taunting the two horror icons to get them, and the closer they got to them, they both tripped over the wires and were tangled together at their feet.

Danny quickly runs over to the power circuit and turns the high voltage to over its maximum peak. Both were electrocuted and exploded. They were eliminated from the game and nowhere to be seen.

The four cheered in victory and the chubby clown man smiled at them.

"It is now over, said them!" in a proud way!

After that was done, they went and looked around to see if there were other students still around and unfortunately there was no one left but only them.

They then decided to head for the exit from the front gate where they went to in the beginning.

They assume it must be reopened because of the elimination of their horror icons. But when they have made it there, unfortunately the gates are still shut tight with chains on it.

They were disappointed and scared, don't know what else to do next to get out of the amusement park. They think they are stuck for the time being.

"The gate doesn't look like it could even be possible to climb across said Michael!" its just high for anybody to reach to.

The four looks confused until the chubby clown man tells them that there might be a possible way out of here in this park.

He showed them the way and followed him with trust.

When they arrived at the location that he told, he showed them to this game room section where none of them or the other students have been to yet.

It was the circus room that looks to have been abandoned many decades ago.

The chubby clown man explains to the four that this show room can lead to the way out of this park and exit out of here.

Something feels very odd to Danny as to how this showroom could lead them out of here. He thinks it's like another tunnel again, but the chubby clown man told him no and that the four should go all the way on top of the raft and make a jump dive down into the pool and escape this terror park.

"Trust me, said the clown man!" rushing them in a way!

So, they all trusted him with their instincts and went all the way to the top of the raft.

When they have finally made it to the top, none of them could see the chubby clown man anywhere from the bottom ground.

"Where did he go, said Jane!" in a very worried and confused way!

They tried calling for him, but he could not be seen anywhere.

All of them walked closer to the edge of the surface to see what the clown man was talking about. And all they see is water, but then for a sudden moment, the water of the pool started to change into inferno flames swirling around into a hell's portal.

"It is a hell's portal not an exit to this amusement park, said Michael!"

Danny knew that there was something very odd about the clown man and that he should not be trusted in the first place.

When they were staring down at the hell's portal, they can suddenly hear a gurgling sound from behind them. They turned around and saw Kayako Saeki!

Jane was the one that was too afraid and couldn't stand it anymore and jumped off the raft down into the hell's portal.

"NO, said Michael!"

Kayako Saeki is getting quite closer to them. Michael was crying in a helpless way and gave up on himself. He too jumps off in the hell's portal.

Jessica can be seen crying, but Danny told her to be strong and stay with him.

Danny yells at Kayako Saeki, "You are dead." You just won't die would you!

Kayako Saeki had paused herself for a moment. Her entire body turns and twitches seeing her changed into somebody else.

The two were surprised to see who it was, and it was Matilda from the school. She was only disguising herself as Kayako Saeki for that very moment.

Matilda told them that she was only her for a while and the real kayako Saeki had already been eliminated by them.

Danny yells at her in a trembling voice asking as to why she is doing this and what did they and all the students do to her that are being sent to hell for what reason!

Before she tells the reason to them, she wanted them to know at first if they realized the two and the rest of the other students that arrived at this amusement park are all already dead by now.

Danny and Jessica look confused as to not know what she is on about.

"Before you'll have arrived here, said Matilda!" did you realized everybody is dead from inside the bus. That's when it occurred. That wasn't sleeping but are dead.

Both looked devastated.

"So that's what happened, said Danny!" Everybody was too fatigued to even realize it. We were all poisoned.

Matilda further explains to them, the two that the reason as to why she did all of this and why she handpicked the students from the school is for revenge!

"What did we do, said Jessica?"

Matilda further explains to them that she was once a beautiful teen girl from their school in the late sixties.

Danny just remembered for a split second that no wonder why everything from this amusement park is all very cheap, the fun fairs and the food.

Matilda continued to explain to them that she was the top one and only prettiest girl from her school and that all the guys fell in love with her and had the girls hated her.

Matilda's hair is always covering her face and then she moves her hair to the side and shows the scar what she looked like to them. Matilda's face has a giant scar on the left side of her cheek. It was cut and sliced by another jealous teen girl from the school with a pair of scissors.

Once that was shown to them, she further asks the two do they know that she is already dead and a spirit.

All the students are chosen here because of the parents, "The sins of the parents!" she repeatedly said!

"Your parents were murderers in my time, Matilda told!" it was your parents who murdered me on top of this raft, pushing me down to the pool where there was no water in it, and I died. Your parents and the others were bullies that picked on me after I became ugly due to the scar on my face, nobody likes me anymore. You are the ones that are now chosen to feel my wrath!

"This time you will be pushed down by me into hells portal and suffer for the rest of eternity, said she!"

Jessica interrupts her trying to talk her out of this by making a deal not to go to hell.

"If I eliminate my own parents because of what they have done to you, said she!" would I be able to avoid going to hell if I avenge your death. It was wrong the way they treated you.

Matilda wasn't quite sure to believe what Jessica had said to her about avenging her death for that moment. She wanted them to feel certain, so she got up closer to the two and showed them the vision of her past.

Danny and Jessica have now seen her vision and understand the pain and suffering that she was in. It was very outrage and intensifying.

They made a promise to avenge her death if Matilda will set them free. Matilda made a deal in one condition, only if they would not just kill their own parents but also the rest of the parents of the other students too that bullied her.

They agreed.

They have until three days to get the job done. Matilda vanishes away from that very spot.

Danny and Jessica looked at each other and didn't really know what to expect the outcome that they are about to do. The two have just witnessed something horrific from the past of their parents.

When they had gotten out of the show room and went straight to the front entrance of the amusement park, the gate is finally opened.

They also see the bus that drove them here which looks to be waiting for them.

The two hopped on the bus and went back into their bodies. The clown bus driver had driven away from the park and headed back to the near school.

While driving, Danny and Jessica went through each one of the students' pockets to reach out for their IDs to find out where they all lived so they could get them later.

Hours later, they arrived back to the location where they were picked up from the start. The two then split up, taking his bike and Jessica took Michael's bike and went in their own separate ways, going back home. They know what they must do next when they head home.

And when Danny arrived first at home feeling exhausted from the amusement park trip, he sees both his mom and dad standing there waiting for him.

His dad asks him is he alright?

Danny didn't answer properly but asks him if he and mom knew who Matilda is back in their younger teen years from the mid-sixties.

Both tried to deny it at first pretending that they don't know who she is and what he was talking about?

Danny got furious as he knows the two are lying. So, he yells at them, and finally confesses.

"Is it true that you guys murdered her, he asks!" back in the time at the amusement park because she was ugly due to the scar on her face.

Yes, they confess that as well.

Danny couldn't stand to know the truth anymore as he witnessed it through the vision, he saw of Matilda being bullied to death.

He walked to the kitchen and took out the knife and went to his mom and dad. He literally stabs them both to death dropping them down to the floor.

After they are dead. He calls on his mobile to speak to Jessica to see what is happening on her side.

She has accomplished exactly like him and is ready to meet up on the next day to go out on a killing spree of the other parents that had messed around with Matilda.

The next following day, one by one the parents were slowly getting killed silently until there is none left.

Their mission is completed. Danny and Jessica have headed back to the amusement park to see Matilda themselves. They travel back there meeting up of their dead parent's car on the next day.

Hours later, they arrived at the park. They went inside to search for Matilda. Danny calls out to her but there was no response at all. She then suddenly appeared behind him.

"Scared the crap out of me, said him!" appeared out of nowhere behind me!

The two will no longer go to hell, she says to them. you did what you promised.

Matilda's spirit fades away as she is now free herself. She gave a nice smile to them in a thankful way and vanished.

"Everything is accomplished, said Danny!" "RIP said Jessica."

The two can be seen hugging each other at that very moment.

While they were hugging each other, Jessica could see from the side a bunch of angry looking people standing there at the front entrance of the gate.

They were the other siblings of the parents that were killed by them. They have been followed all the way here.

The two had made the mistake by not eliminating the other siblings and now they have all gathered around to kill the two. They're outnumbered.

"But how did most of them know that it was us, said Jessica?"

"There must be surveillance cameras, said Danny!"

"We are now definitely screwed aren't we, said he!

The siblings looked very upset and charged at the two.

"This is the end of the both of us, said Jess!" holding each other in fear.

They set Matilda's soul free while Danny and Jessica are about to be slaughtered by them.

 "It is not fair, said Jess!"

Then for a sudden the siren came on in the amusement park. Everybody stood still and looked confused. The siblings didn't know what the siren was for. The siren stops at that very moment.

The chubby clown man and a bunch of work attendants gather around the area surrounding all the siblings with weapons exactly like they're holding onto.

Danny and Jessica looked to be surprised to see the chubby clown man again. They thought that he had left them for good. Both parties attacked each other.

While they were fighting, the chubby clown man grabbed Danny and Jessica out of it and bring them into a much safer place.

The two thanked him and thought that it was the last time that they would see him. They also thought he was the bad guy as well but thought wrong until just now.

Jessica asks him what's his actual name is, as they keep referring to him as a clown man. He then told them that his name is Choppa chop!

"Isn't that a lollipop name, Danny says!"

The two thanked him for saving them from the brawl.

"don't mentioned it, said Choppa chop!" Thank you to you two for helping my daughter.

They couldn't believe for a split second that Matilda had been his daughter all along.

Choppa chop also made a confession to them, explaining that he was supposed to help his daughter eliminate all the students including them too from the very start. Because of a deal that they made to his daughter, he decided to help them out. He too is a spirit!

For everything to be done, Matilda is now reborn as a girl again and for the father, he too will be reborn as her father once more.

He had explained everything they needed to know and said their final goodbye. He vanishes away!

Then for that very moment, Michael and Jane reappeared out of nowhere all the sudden. It must be Choppa chop's heart that set them free from hell.

They were all happy to have seen each other.

About the deaths of Michael and Jane's parents, they knew what happen while being in hell. They saw everything and agreed to what they had done. And that's why they have been set free from hells world back to earth.

The four walked out of the amusement park and disappeared out into the world where unknown. All the siblings are killed off by the attendance. While they were going, they were wondering why everybody's parents were all much younger looking than they are. "Big mystery, they all said!" might be a curse from Matilda and Choppa chop!

The End